The Berenstain Bears
DON'T POLLUTE
⟨ ANYMORE ⟩

When Bear Country's cubs
learn pollution's a fact,
they help grownups learn
to clean up their act.

A First Time Book®

The Berenstain Bears
DON'T POLLUTE
⟨ ANYMORE ⟩

Stan & Jan Berenstain

Random House 🏠 New York

Library of Congress Cataloging-in-Publication Data:
Berenstain, Stan.   The Berenstain bears don't pollute (anymore) / Stan & Jan Berenstain.   p.   cm. — (A First time book)   SUMMARY: The bears in Bear Country grow concerned about how pollution and waste of natural resources are damaging the world around them, so they form The Earthsavers Club.   ISBN 0-679-82351-4 (pbk.) — ISBN 0-679-92351-9 (lib. bdg.)   [1. Pollution—Fiction.   2. Conservation of natural resources—Fiction.   3. Bears—Fiction.]   I. Berenstain, Jan.   II. Title.   III. Series: Berenstain, Stan.   First time books.   PZ7.B4483Benb   1991   [E]—dc20   91-9147

Manufactured in the United States of America   10 9 8 7 6 5 4 3 2 1

"Oh?" said Brother and Sister Bear, coming to see.

"There's a big story, too," said Papa, "and a headline."

"My goodness," said Mama Bear. "What's it about?"

"'Leading scientist claims Bear Country is in serious trouble,'" he said, reading the headline.

"What sort of trouble?" asked Sister.

Papa, who was reading the story to himself, didn't answer.

"What *sort* of trouble?" said Mama, repeating Sister's question.

"Oh, you know how professors are," he said. "Actual Factual's making a big fuss about pollution."

"Well, I know how Professor Actual Factual is," said Mama, "and I think he's quite sensible."

"So do I," said Sister.

"Me too," agreed Brother.

"Oh, he's a great guy, all right," said Papa. "He's dug up some terrific dinosaur bones, and he runs a great museum. But I happen to think he's gone a little overboard on this pollution thing. I'm as much against pollution as the next fellow," he continued. "I just don't think a couple of candy wrappers and drinking cups along the side of the road is the end of the world."

"Besides, Bear Country is in great shape. Come on, I'll show you." He opened the door and led the family out onto the front stoop. "You see? Bear Country is not only in good shape, it's downright beautiful: the rolling hills, the forests, the lakes and streams—and just look at that sunset!"

"It's beautiful, all right," agreed Brother. "But our science book says that some of those colors are caused by chemicals in the air that shouldn't be there."

"Piffle!" said Papa. "Say, aren't you two supposed to be doing homework?"

Sister, who had just about completed her homework, finished quickly. But Brother Bear was stuck. Teacher Bob had asked him to do a report on endangered species. The books he had taken out of the school library weren't very helpful.

Of course, the kind of shape Bear Country was in wasn't as simple as Papa made it seem. How Bear Country looked depended on your point of view. It looked fine from the Bear family's front stoop. It looked even better if you had a bird's-eye view while flying high above the earth.

But if you had a squirrel's-eye view and were finding fewer and fewer acorns because too many trees were being cut down, Bear Country didn't look so fine. If you had a duck's-eye view, you might think the professor was right about pollution. And if you had a fish's-eye view, you might think things were downright awful!

The next day Brother decided to visit the museum to ask Professor Actual Factual for help with his endangered species report. Sister Bear went with him.

BEARSONIAN INSTITUTION

Professor Actual Factual was usually cheerful and friendly and bubbling over with ideas and projects when the cubs visited, but this time he looked worried and glum. He cheered up a bit when he saw them, but when Brother told him the purpose of the visit—to get help on a report about endangered species—he said something very surprising. "I'll tell you the endangered species to do your report on—US!"

"We don't understand," they said.
"It's very simple," explained the
professor. "We bears and all other
creatures need certain things to
survive: clean air to breathe,
pure water to drink, and good
soil to grow food in. If we
don't do something about
pollution, we're all going
to become endangered
species.

"Come," he said, "you'll understand soon enough." He led them out to where the Actual-Factualmobile was parked. It was a special van with all kinds of scientific gear in it.

ACTUAL-FACTUALMOBILE

Then the professor took Brother and Sister on a Bear Country tour they wouldn't soon forget.

They went past Grizzly Gus's Garage, where they saw oil leaking into a stream, getting on a duck, and killing some fish. They went past the old box factory, where they saw ugly black smoke pouring into the air.

They scuba-dived into Great Bear Lake, where they saw everything from soda cans to rusty old bedsprings—and worse! They saw a fish tangled in a plastic soda-can holder! They cut it loose, but they couldn't rescue *all* the fish from all the plastic holders carelessly thrown away.

They drove through the forest and saw that a great many trees had been cut down, and that not many new trees had been planted to replace them.

"You might speak to your dad about that," said the professor. "He and his fellow woodsbears could help with that problem."

"I think I see what you mean about becoming an endangered species," said Brother when they got back to the museum.

"Yes," agreed Sister, "but what are we going to *do* about it?!"

"Did that *Evening News* story do much good?" asked Brother.

"Not much," said the professor. "The idea that Bear Country is in serious trouble because of pollution seems to be hard to get across."

"To *grownups*, maybe," said Sister. "But *we* understand, and all our cub friends will, too. Because *we're* the ones who'll have to live on a messed-up, polluted earth when we grow up!"

"Professor," said Brother, "how does this sound? You come to our school and explain all about pollution to the cubs of Bear Country. Maybe *we* can do something about it!"

Actual Factual was impressed. "I'll give Teacher Bob a call right away and arrange it," he said.

And that's what happened. The cubs were all eyes and ears as Actual Factual told them about the trouble Bear Country was getting into. First, he taught them three important new words: *ecology, conservation,* and *recycle.* The way the professor explained it, *ecology* means how all the creatures, the plants, and the earth itself work together. *Conservation* means not wasting the valuable things of the earth—like water, oil, wood, and metal. And *recycle* means finding ways to use some of those valuable things over and over.

The cubs learned quite a lot from Actual Factual, and they had some ideas of their own, too.

"How about a recycling program?" suggested one cub.

"Maybe for newspapers to start," added another, "then, if it works— for cans and bottles, too." Tim Honeypot said he'd talk to his dad, Mayor Honeypot, about it.

Brother Bear remembered Grizzly Gus's Garage. "You shouldn't be allowed to spill oil into streams and kill fish," he said.

Babs Bruno, whose dad was the chief of police, said, "I'll talk to my dad. If there isn't a law against it, there ought to be."

Even Too-Tall helped with an idea.
"My uncle owns the Super-Duper Market.
He could put in a bag-return plan for
reusing bags."

"Excellent suggestion," said the professor.
"And if some folks don't wanna cooperate,"
added Too-Tall, "me and the gang can lean
on 'em a little."
"The bag-return is fine, Too-Tall,"
said Teacher Bob, "but *no leaning*!"

Cousin Freddy had the best idea of all.
"Let's start a club to stop pollution
and call it the Earthsavers Club.
We'll make posters and bumper
stickers and have cleanups
and marches and parades!"
But there was still the problem of
Papa and his fellow woodsbears.

That evening Brother and Sister told Mama and Papa about the Earthsavers Club and all the plans for stopping pollution. Mama was very impressed. Papa was too. "As I said before, I'm just as much against pollution as the next fellow!" But when the cubs asked him to be sure that he and his fellow woodsbears plant a new tree for every one they cut down, he got a little grumpy.

"Humph!" he grumped. "It's hard enough to cut trees down without having to plant them as well. Besides, what's all the fuss about? They're just trees!"

"My dear," said Mama, "the cubs are right. The forest is a living thing and deserves respect." Papa was about to say "Piffle!" but thought better of it.

The problem of conserving the forest must
have been on his mind, because that night
he had a dream. In the dream he was walking toward
the forest to cut wood—when the trees began to sway
and wave their branches! Then the branches turned
into reaching, grasping arms. Then the
trees climbed out of the earth on their
roots and chased him.

"Help!" cried terrified Papa in his sleep. "The trees! They're after me!" He woke up in a cold sweat.

"Having a nightmare?" asked Mama.
"Er—it must have been something I ate,"
he said.

"Or something you heard, perhaps?"
she said. *"About trees?"*

"Piffle!" he said, and turned
over to try to go back to sleep.
But it wasn't going to be easy.

The cubs didn't expect to solve all of Bear Country's pollution problems, but the Earthsavers Club made a very good start.

The mayor declared a special holiday called
Earthsavers Day, and the cubs had a big parade.
Brother and Sister Bear marched at the head
with Professor Actual Factual.

There were many grownups
in the parade, too, including
Papa Bear, who carried a sign
that did *not* say "Piffle."